MISSION :-
AYURVEDIC SANATAN HINDU RASHTRA AKHAND BHARAT / VISHWA - 2050

Title : Mission - Ayurvedic Sanatan Hindu Rashtra Akhand
Bharat/Vishwa -2050

Author : Kanhaiya Jee Anand

Edition : 1st (January, 2024)

ISBN : 9788196784683

Published by

Regd. Add.: 254, Khuriyakhatta No. 10, Bindukhatta,
Lalkuan, Nainital - 262402, Uttarakhand, India
Website : www.taneeshapublishers.in
E-mail : taneeshapublishers@gmail.com
Phone : +91 845481 2712, +91 976041 7980

Printed by :

Manipal Technologies Limited, Bengaluru - 560001, Karnataka

WRITTEN BY-

Mr. Kanhaiya Jee Anand, AMIE, MBA
Ms. Bedatri Anand, B.Arch
Mrs. Sharda Kumari, MA (Human Rights)
Mr. Utakars Anand, B Arch

Flat No-603, Block-A, Astha Green City, AIIMS ROAD,
Phulwari, Patna, Bihar - 801505
At- Hasanpur, Lakhisarai, Bihar-811311
Mobile No - 9204783656, 9263303481

DEDICATION

Dedicated to our Mother Devotee of Krishna
Mrs.Draupdi Devi and all family members.

Special Dedication to our RSS family
Patna, Team of Engineer Live Foundation,
Sar Sangh Chalak Sri Mohan Bhagwat Ji,
Budhaavtar Jagatguru Sankracharya Puripith
and Sant Jai Mangla Baba.

भारत माता
उत्तरं यत् समुद्रस्य हिमाद्रैश्चैव दक्षिणम्।
वर्षं तत् भारतं नाम भारती यत्र संततिः।।
विष्णु पुराण (स्कंध-२, श्लोक-३)
BHARAT MATA

INDEX

Preface

Akhand Bharat is the mission of every Bhartiya.

It is said in Vishnu Purana :-

उत्तरं यत्समुद्रस्य: हिमाद्रेश्चैव दक्षिणम् ।

वर्षं तद् भारतं नाम: भारती यत्र संततिः ।।

The country (varam) that lies north of the ocean and south of the snowy mountains is called Bhāratam; there dwell the descendants of Bharata."

Barhaspatya Shastra says:-

हिमालयं समारभ्य: यावत् इंदु सरोवरं।

तं देवनिर्मितं देशं हिंदुस्थानं प्रचक्षते।।

Starting from the Himalayas and extending up to the Indian Ocean is the nation built by Gods, Hindusthan.

MEANING OF AKHAND BHARAT

Akhand Bharat is not the dream but this is essential to appen, immagine hen the Indian Continent and Australia divided from the African Continent and Indian Continent pushed to Asia and the Australian Continent stabilized in different parts. Indian Continents have various country is attached is that Bharat, Iran, UAE, Oman, Arab, Afghanistan, Pakistan, Bharat, Bangladesh, Nepal, Bhutan, Tibet, SriLanka, Maldives, Myanmar, Laos, Thailand, Vietnam & Others.

Bharat is the main country who can lead the all above country which is divided as per time and irregular development.

Bringing together the above country is the prime requirement of the Ayurvedic Sanatan Hindu Rastra Bharat.

All the above countries have a good relation with the Bharat and all countries depending on utilization of Ayurveda and sanatan parampara, hence this is the Indian thought which can create the Akhand Bharat to just create a specific mission.

Every system must have its own discipline to run the country in the right direction.

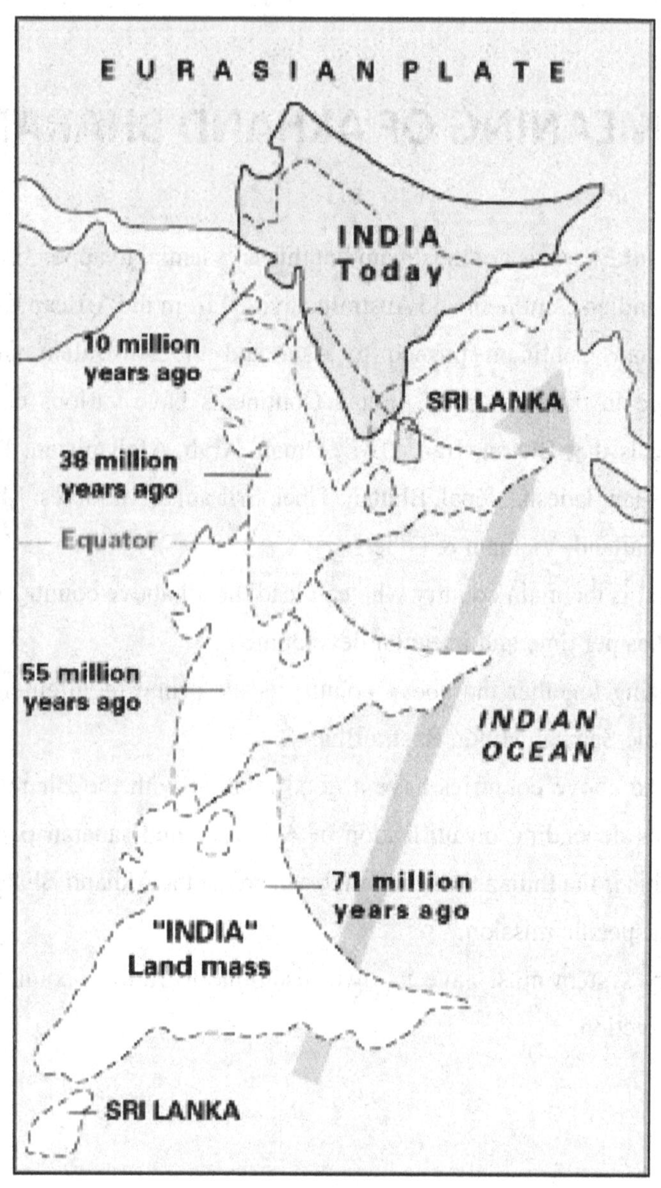

Ayurvedic Sanatan Hindu Rastra Akhand Bharat: United Bharat

This one word is enough to describe the Dream of Every Hindu.

This is How Akhand Bharat looks like

This is, Typically the Map Where Hindus Were in Majority before Other Religions Come

isn't it good? Yes, it's Marvelous.

This is the Map of Ayurvedic Sanatan Hindu Akhand Bharat, and also the map of **Bharatvarsh/Aryavarta** *that is mentioned in Hindu Scriptures, mainly in Puranas.*

According to the Scriptures.

It is said in Vishnu Purana :-

उत्तरं यत्समुद्रस्यः हिमाद्रेश्चैव दक्षिणम् ।

वर्षं तद् भारतं नामः भारती यत्र संततिः ।।

The country (varam) that lies north of the ocean and south of the snowy mountains is called Bhāratam; there dwell the descendants of Bharata. "

Barhaspatya Shastra says:-

हिमालयं समारभ्यः यावत् इंदु सरोवरं ।

तं देवनिर्मितं देशं हिंदुस्थानं प्रचक्षते ।।

Starting from the Himalayas and extending up to the Indian Ocean is the nation built by Gods, Hindusthan.

This Land is the Most Pure and Divine Place as per Hinduism.

*This Land gave us many Religions like **Hinduism, Buddhism, Jainism, Sikhism.** These Religions are also known as Dharmic Religions since they work on the Principles of Ayurvedic Sanatan Parampara.*

There are many Great Kings from India who Ruled over the Majority of the Parts of the Indian Subcontinent.

We are in part of Bharat, no doubt, Bharat means Joint Bharat, Iran, UAE, Oman, Arab, Afghanistan, Pakistan, Bharat, Bangladesh, Nepal, Bhutan, Tibet, SriLanka, Maldives, Myanmar, Laos, Thailand, Vietnam & Others.

This is the stage which ask, why Akhand Bharat.

Why Akhand Bharat

During the Indian independence movement, Kanaiyalal Maneklal Munshi advocated for Akhand Bharat, a proposition that Mahatma Gandhi agreed with, believing that as Britain wanted to retain their empire by pursuing a policy of divide and rule, Hindu–Muslim unity could not be achieved as long as the British were there. In addition, Mazhar Ali Khan wrote that "the Khan brothers [were] determined to fight for Akhand Bharat, and challenged the League to fight the issue out before the electorate of the Province. On 7–8 October 1944, in Delhi, Radha Kumud Mukherjee presided over the Akhand Bharat Leaders' Conference.

The Indian activist and Hindu Mahasabha leader Vinayak Damodar Savarkar at the Hindu Mahasabha's 19th Annual Session in Ahmedabad in 1937 propounded the notion of an Akhand Bharat that "must remain one and indivisible" "from Kashmir to Rameswaram, from Sindh to Assam. " He said that "all citizens who owe undivided loyalty and allegiance to the Bharat nation and to the Indian state shall be treated with perfect equality and shall share duties and obligations equally in common, irrespective of caste, creed or religion, and the representation also shall either be on the basis of one man one vote or in proportion to the population in case of separate electorates and public services shall go by merit alone.

The call for creation of the Akhand Bharat or Akhand Bharat has on occasions been raised by Hindu nationalist organizations such as the Hindu Mahasabha, Rashtriya Swayamsevak Sangh, Vishva Hindu Parishad, Shiv Sena, Maharashtra Navnirman Sena, Hindu Sena, Hindu

Janajagruti Samiti, Bharatiya Janata Party, Engineer Live Foundation etc. One organization sharing this goal, the Akhand Bharat Morcha, bears the term in its name.

Pre-1947 maps of India, showing the modern states of Pakistan and Bangladesh as part of British India illustrate the borders of a proto-Akhand Bharat. The creation of an Akhand Bharat is also ideologically linked with the concept of Hindutva (Hindu nationalism) and the ideas of sangathan (unity) and shuddhi (purification).

When Britisher was leaving the Bhartiya Continents then he prepared guidelines which should be followed by the countries like Bharat, Pakistan, Bangladesh, Sri Lanka, Nepal, Bhutan, Burma, Afghanistan, Tibbat, Vietnam, Laos, Malaysia etc. Now Akhand Bharat is only possible when other countries will join us on their own.

Countries can Join by STRONG DEMOCRACY only.

Can we ask, what is the meaning of STRONG DEMOCRACY?

The Democracy who follow the strong discipline of Sixteen Sanskar.

There is limitation and hindrances behind has to talk now.

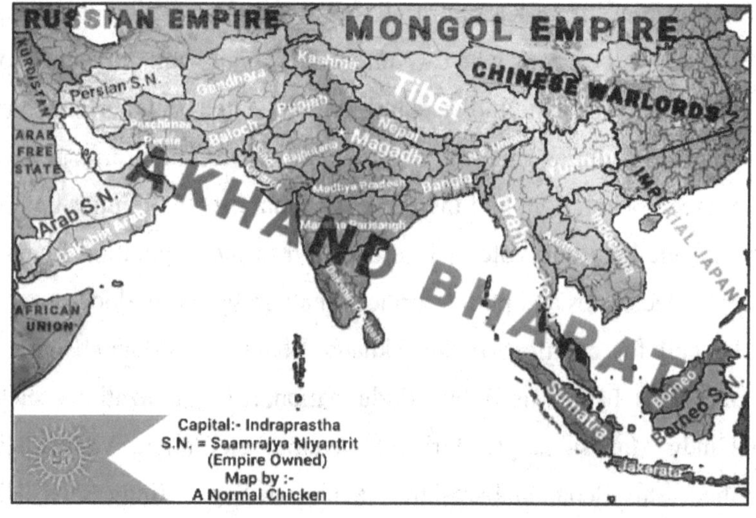

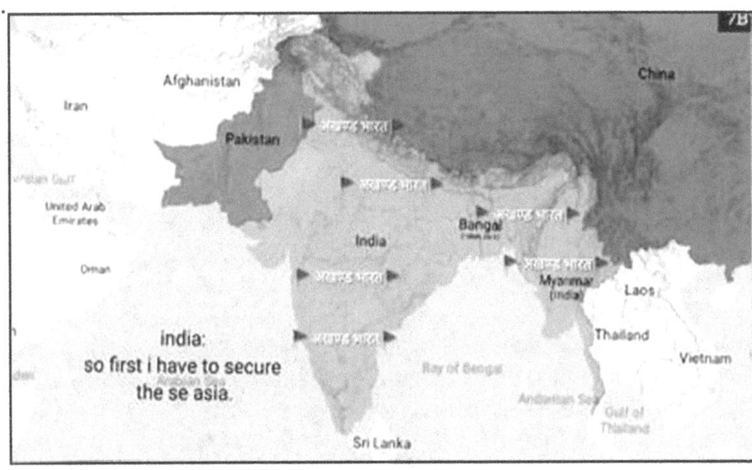
Pakistan-occupied Kashmir
Aksai Chin - captured by China
कब-कब बंटा भारत...
(History of when India was divided)
अफगानिस्तान 1876
Afghanistan
पाकिस्तान 1947
Pakistan
कश्मीर 1948
अक्साई चीन
चीन का कब्जा 1962
जम्मू कश्मीर
Jammu & Kashmir
तिब्बत 1914
Tibet
नेपाल 1964
Nepal
Bhutan
(15 August)
15 अगस्त
अखण्ड भारत
("Undivided India")
Bangladesh
ब्रह्मदेश (म्यान्मार) 1937
Burma
("Day of Determination", or "Oath Day")
सकल्प-दिवस
हर साधु भक्त का स्वप्न
(Every patriot's dream)
Sri Lanka

Afghanistan
Iran
Pakistan
China
United Arab Emirates
Oman
India
अखण्ड भारत
अखण्ड भारत
अखण्ड भारत
अखण्ड भारत
अखण्ड भारत
अखण्ड भारत
Bangal
Myanmar (India)
Laos
Thailand
Vietnam
Bay of Bengal
Andaman Sea
Gulf of Thailand
india: so first i have to secure the se asia.
Sri Lanka

VIKRAMADITYA

What are Some Negative Aspects of Akhand Bharat?

Akhand Bharat isn't a Good Idea at this Point

In this Answer, I will try to explain to you that Akhand Bharat is not a Good idea, and we shouldn't focus on that. and I will try to cover many other aspects too.

*Now some people might be wondering how **This Country Broke into so many parts.***

Answer:

The country which you are seeing on the map come Together during

- ***Chankya***
- ***Pandava***
- ***Bikramaditya***
- ***Britishers***

Although this whole country united only a few times. but they were Ruled by Hindu Kings in Ancient Times.

This Map will give an Idea that how and When these Countries are Divided

Now the Question Arises

What's the Problem in Making Akhand Bharat?

Answer:

*The Areas Included in this Map are **India, Pakistan, Bangladesh, Nepal, Bhutan, Myanmar, Sri Lanka, Maldives, Afghanistan, Thailand, Cambodia, Indonesia, and Some Parts of TIBET.***

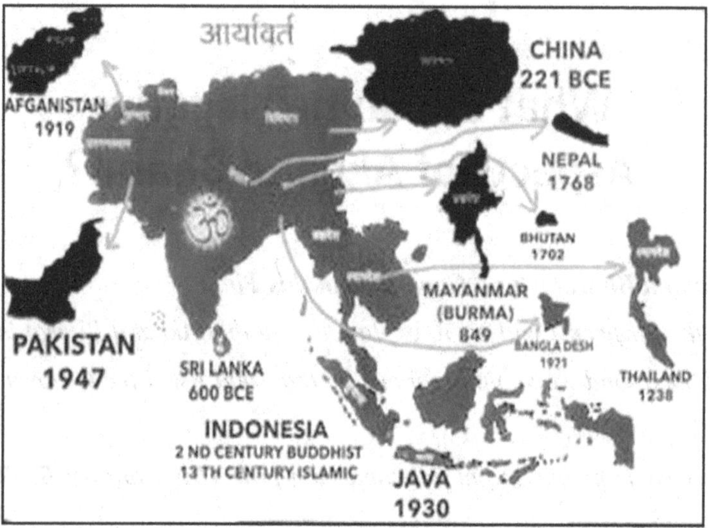

Here I'm going to mention Some Important Problems That We will face by Making Akhand Bharat.

Problems Before Making Akhand Bharat:

- India has to deal with 2 Nuclear Powers namely China and Pakistan. and it seems to be the worst idea to go for a full-fledged war with these 2 countries.

- It also depends on whether the people from the countries that I have mentioned above even want to join with India or Not. Because if they don't want to join with us then there will be some major Civil Wars that will happen across these Countries and groups of People.

- Getting International Recognition will be hard because many people throughout the world will not accept this and this may even harm the image of Bharat on the International Stage.

- If Bharat somehow succeeds in making Akhand Bharat then there are a lot of Chances that some fringe elements will again try to Separate our Country.

Problems After Making Akhand Bharat:

1. Over-Population: *We all are aware that Bharat is the Ist Largest Country in terms of Populations, and just think of what will happen when we add all the countries that I have mentioned above?*

Now Let's just Try to Calculate the Population of the Newly Formed Country.

Bharat: 1. 38 billion

Pakistan: 220 million

Bangladesh: 164 million

Afghanistan: 40 million

Nepal: 3 million

Sri Lanka: 21 million

Bhutan: 700k

Myanmar: 54 million

Thailand: 70 million

Indonesia: 273 million

Cambodia: 16 million

Tibet: 3. 5 million

Now if we add the Population of all these countries then We get it as

The population of Akhand Bharat: 2. 24+Billion People

*There are about **7. 9 billion** people on this Planet Earth and the Population of Akhand Bharat will be around **2. 24 billion**. This means **Every 3rd Human will be from Akhand Bharat**. This sounds Great but with a lot of Population comes a lot of problems too. and **no government or police in the World can Handle this much of Population.***

2. Demography

This is gonna be the Core Problem for Those who Dream for Akhand Bharat. Let me Give the Data of 2. 24 billion people religion-wise.

Hindus: 1. 3 Billion *(About 1 billion in India and rest from other countries)*

Islam: 1. 1 Billion

Buddhism: 100 million

Christian: 60 million

I calculated The following Data with so many approximations so there can be errors too, please ignore that.

The Demography Factor is gonna be the biggest problem because the remaining people will hardly accept their roots and this will become the biggest backslash for Hindus.

3. Governance

Controlling a Population of around 2. 24 billion people isn't a joke, it will be the toughest challenge for the Government to Control such a Big Population and maintain law and Order.

We can think of other forms of government like the Decentralization of Government, or else it will be so hard for a single leader to control such a big Country.

4. Unemployment

Unemployment is gonna be a key factor in the Failure of Akhand Bharat, as all these countries are now united then people will have to run for jobs because. Take this example. There is a company X in Thailand who needs labor for their Company then they will prefer it from India because Indian Labour workforce can work at lower wages too, and not only that there are many such problems that will lead to Unemployment such as Increase in Competition, more number of people will apply for jobs but hardly few will get it due to unavailability of seats, and various other factors.

5. Migrations

Migration problem will increase so much and there will be a lot of

Empty places at some States and Some states will get overcrowded,

For example: if Indians get to know that there are very cheap and affordable houses available in Myanmar then many people will storm towards Myanmar, and there will be a lot of Places that soon will turn into a ghost city in India and at the same time these people will start overcrowding in Myanmar. and vice-versa.

Problems We Should Focus on Our Country:

1. Unemployment

This is one of the Biggest Problems that we need to focus on first in our Country, During the lockdown, millions of people lost their jobs. our main focus must be increasing the Job opportunities and not only providing jobs but proper Wages too. Millions of Indians who have a job are underpaid, they don't get enough money even for Food. and it's high time we should focus on both providing jobs with proper wages.

2. Development

Even though the government is doing a lot in the Development sectors, still we lack behind in many sectors. The rate at which India is developing is gonna take around 20–30y more for India to be considered as a Developed country. so the Indian Government should also focus on Developing at a Faster Rate.

3. Border Dispute

We share our Borders with **Pakistan, Bangladesh, Nepal, Myanmar, Bhutan, and Tibet.**

but there are 2 countries that are the biggest headache for India they are **Pakistan and China.** *These two countries always start some border disputes with India and India also fought many wars and there is some kind of Cold wars going on within these Countries. and The Clash between them is a topic of concern for the whole world and not just India, China,*

Pakistan but also the whole world because these 3 countries have Nuclear Power, and we all know how Dangerous these Weapons are and they have the power to wipe out the population of the Whole world with just one click.

4. We should focus on re-capturing Aksai-chin and POK from China and Pakistan respectively. It's been a very long time since China and Pakistan forcefully Captured these areas, and till now they are not giving it back, so why ain't we try to take it back?

These are some of my Viewpoints on What all Indians must Know and should think of its other consequences before Thinking of Akhand Bharat.

Although I'm do use the Akhand Bharat in memes or some other places and yes this is my dream and we all want that this dream may come true but its consequences are scarier than not having an Akhand Bharat.

Now time has come to talk about the Strong Democracy and Strong Discipline System.

Why Akhand Bharat needs Democratic Bharat

In Present condition of the world, Raj Tantra can not rule, as people got the education. In this condition Democracy is the only one solution to rule the country. A Strong Democracy with their **"STRONG DISCIPLINE SYSTEM"** can win any World.

What does **" Strong Democracy"** mean?

Democracy is the one system which is for the People by the people and has a special Discipline.

Democracy is such a system of governance, under which the public can choose their representative by voting for any candidate who has voluntarily come to the election , and can make him a member of the legislature. Democracy is made up of two words, "Lok + Tantra".

Lok means people and Tantra means governance.

Although the term is used in a political context, the principle of democracy is relevant to other groups and organizations as well.

Basically, democracy is a mixture of different principles, democracy is the rule of the people, by the people and for the people.

There is such a system in a democracy that the public can choose the legislature as per their wish.

Democracy is a type of governance, in which all people have equal rights.

A good democracy is one in which there is a system of economic justice along with political and social justice.

This system of governance in the country provides social, political and religious freedom to the people.

Every system develops with the different different discipline.

But Democracy developing with the Panchsheel Discipline described in Upanishad ist developed in Vaishali State.

Vaishali State who strengthened the Democracy to strictly follow the 18 Sanskar, Four Ashram Life and Navdha Bhakti (Nine Work)

Now the question Is arising Is as under-

What is Ayurvedic Sanatan Hindu Rashtra parampara?

Sanatan Parampara is depends on three useful concept or discipline is as under. -

I. Practical Knowledge of 16 Sanskar.

II. Practical Knowledge of Four Ashrams Life and

III. Practical Knowledge of Navdha Bhakti (Nine Work)

What is Democratic Bharat?

Ayurvedic Sanatan Hindu Rastra Bharat depends on Strong Democracy.

Democracy is the backbone of Society. The system develops at various stages of development as per the situation of Life and various systems developing to run the society.

In world either the Country is called ISLAMIC OR CHRISTIAN OR COMMUNIST OR BUDDHIST. This Country have own discipline to follow. Ayurvedic Sanatan Hindu Rasta Bharat is the Ist Rastra in World has strong vision of Democracy and following the Discipline of 16 Sanskar, four stage Life and Navdha Bhakti (Nine Work).

Various system such as Troop or Criminal or Gunda Tantra (Troop Cracy or Crimocracy or Gundacracy), FamilyTantra (FamilyCracy), KisanTantra (FarmerCracy), TradeTantra (TradeCracy), CasteTantra (CasteCracy), TechnicalTantra (Technocracy), SanatanTantra (Santan Parampara), Community Tantra (Community Cracy), Societal Tantra (Societal Cracy), Village Tantra (Village Cracy), Panchayat Tantra (Panchayat Cracy), Jila Tantra (Jila Cracy), State Tantra (State Cracy), Raj Tantra (KingCracy), Praja Tantra (Democracy) have own discipline and performing in same discipline.

Every Tantra has its own discipline to run with limitations while Democracy has discipline which allows all people to participate in Government Formation. Discipline of Democracy disallowing the limitation of all other Tantra.

Learning and Following of Panchsheel is the prime of Democracy which is essential to learn before the start of education in School or Gurukul by the UPNAYAN SANSKAR or INITIATION ACTIVITY.

What is SANATAN PARAMPARA (HINDUISM) & DISCIPLINE

SANATAN have the option to follow all chapters of GITA from 1 to 18 from Birth to Death in different different stages. Sanatan people follow the 16 Sanskar, which comes in different phases of life which includes the 18 chapter of GITA.

There are Nine works divided which indicate to perform any work with devotion, that work will give peace to the concerned People.

Sacred Sixteen Sacraments of Hinduism (SANATAN)

Hinduism(Sanatan) is the theme of India. In this, sixteen sacred rites are performed.

Due to the antiquity and vastness of Hinduism, it is also called 'Sanatan Dharma'.

SANATAN(Hinduism), like Buddhism, Jainism, Christianity, Islam, etc. , is not a Community established by any particular person, but a large set of different communities and beliefs that have been going on since ancient times.

According to Maharishi Ved Vyas, sixteen sacred sacraments are performed from birth to death.

Which is as follows :-

(1). Conception ceremony, (2). Punsavan rituals. (3). Seemantonnayan Sanskar, (4). Jatkarma Sanskar, (5). Naming Ceremony, (6). The evacuation ceremony, (7). Annaprashan Sanskar, (8) Chudakarma Sanskar, (9). Vidyarambha Sanskar, (10. Karnavedha Sanskar, (11). Yagyopaveet

Sanskar, (12). Vedarambh Sanskar, (13). Keshant Sanskar, (14). Samvartan Sanskar, (15). Marriage & Economic rites, (16). Funeral rites.

1. Garbhadhana-samskara (Conception): Maharishi Charak has said that it is necessary for pregnancy to be happy and strong in the mind, that is why men and women should always eat the answer food and remain happy always.

At the time of conception, the mind of man and woman should be filled with enthusiasm, happiness and health.

In order to get a good child, first of all, conception-sanskar has to be done.

Pregnancy is produced by the combination of Raj and Semen of the parents. This coincidence is called conception.

The physical union of a man and a woman is called garbhadhana-samskara.

After pregnancy, there are attacks of many types of natural defects, to avoid which this sanskar is performed.

By which the pregnancy remains safe.

Good and suitable progeny are produced from the insemination done with proper rituals.

An Ayurvedic Hospital at Village level is essential to help the every individual for the above Sanskar.

2. Punsavan: : Punsavan Sanskar is organized after three months because the brain of the fetus starts developing after three months in the womb.

At this time, the foundation of the sanskars of the child born in the womb is laid through the Punsavan Sanskar.

According to the belief, the child starts learning in the womb, an example of this is Abhimanyu who had received the education of Chakravyuha in the womb of mother Subhdra.

This is the responsibility of every society to develop the Social health

centre where Pregnant ladies can get help to develop.

3. Seemantonnayan- Seemantonnayan Sanskar is performed in the fourth, sixth and eighth months of pregnancy.

At this time the child growing in the womb becomes capable of learning.

To bring knowledge of good qualities, nature and deeds, the mother has to behave in the right way. .

During this, the mother should study by staying calm and happy.

4. Jatakram:

By performing Jatkarma Sanskar as soon as the child is born, many types of defects of the child are removed.

When Child takes birth at that time the child is not taking any breadth and in a few seconds the child starts to take breadth and the family enjoys that occasions.

Under this, on the sixth day the baby is licked with honey and ghee, as well as Vedic mantras are recited so that the child is healthy and long.

On the basis of Jyotish Science Jatakarma is performed for a born child, this Sanskar helps families to train the Child in the same field for better development and benefit to the Society.

In the Present World, mostly children take birth in hospitals, hence the Hospital and their mother father know the Date of Birth, hence this is the responsibility of all Parents and Government to train the human being as per their quality.

Now the question arises, what should be the type of human being?

There are four qualities of human beings as Brahmin, Kshtriya, Vaishya and Shudra.

The Land is also of four similar qualities, Nature also has four similar qualities.

Quality	Brahmin	Kshatriya	Vaishya	Shudra
Land	Brahmin (White Soil)	Kshatriya (Hilly Area)	Vaishya (Mix Soil)	Shudra (Black Soil)
Nature	Brahmin (12AM to 6 AM) & 4PM to 6 PM)	Kshatriya (6AM to 12 PM)	Vaishya (12 PM to 4 PM)	Shudra (6PM to 12 AM)
Human Being	Brahmin (Thinker and who is working for Country)	Kshatriya (Force, Army)	Vaishya (Businessman)	Shudra (Serving to anyone)

Work	Brahmin (Teaching, Research) Income from accepting DAN.	Kshatriya (Safety) Income from accepting Taxes.	Vaishya (Business) Income from Profit.	Shudra (Helping others) Income from Salary.

Types of Human being is as under-

Place of Birth and nature is the primary concern.

Example any children born in Ganga or Gandak region where its soil is white is of Brahmin is always a powerful tool which Creates major quality in children whether they are born as a brahmin, Kshtriya , Vaishya and Shudra.

Nature is another important feature which changes the quality of children. Suppose any child born in the morning 2. 30am to 6am before sunrise, will get the quality of Brahmin.

Similarly following quality is as under-

1. **Brahmin-Brahmin-Brahmin-Brahmin**
2. Brahmin-Brahmin-Brahmin-Kshtriya
3. Brahmin-Brahmin-Brahmin-Vaishya
4. Brahmin-Brahmin-Brahmin-Shudra
5. Brahmin-Brahmin-Kshtriya-Brahmin
6. Brahmin-Brahmin-vaishya-Brahmin
7. Brahmin-Brahman-Shudra-Brahmin
8. Brahmin-Brahmin-Kshtriya-Kshtriya
9. Brahmin-Brahmin-Vaishya-Kshtriya
10. Brahmin-Brahmin-Shudra-Kshtriya
11. Brahmin-Brahmin-Kshtriya-Vaishya
12. Brahmin-Brahmin-Vaishya-Vaishya

13. Brahmin-Brahmin-Shudra-Vaishya
14. Brahmin-Brahmin-Kshtriya-Shudra
15. Brahmin-Brahmin-Vaishya-Shudra
16. Brahmin-Brahmin-Shudra-Shudra
17. Brahmin-Kshtriya-Brahmin-Brahmin
18. Brahmin-Kshtriya-Brahmin-Kshtriya
19. Brahmin-Kshtriya-Brahmin-Vaishya
20. Brahmin-Kshtriya-Brahmin-Shudra
21. Brahmin-Kshtriya-Kshtriya-Brahmin
22. Brahmin-Kshtriya-Kshtriya-Kshtriya
23. Brahmin-Kshtriya-Kshtriya-Vaishya
24. Brahmin-Kshtriya-Kshtriya-Shudra
25. Brahmin-Kshtriya-Vaishya-Brahmin
26. Brahmin-Kshtriya-Vaishya-Kshtriya
27. Brahmin-Kshtriya-Vaishya-Vaishya
28. Brahmin-Kshtriya-Vaishya-Shudra
29. Brahmin-Kshtriya-Shudra-Brahmin
30. Brahmin-Kshtriya-Shudra-Kshtriya
31. Brahmin-Kshtriya-Shudra-Vaishya
32. Brahmin-Kshtriya-Shudra-Shudra
33. Brahmin-Vaishya-Brahmin-Brahmin
34. Brahmin-Vaishya-Brahmin-Kshtriya
35. Brahmin-Vaishya-Brahmin-Vaishya
36. Brahmin-Vaishya-Brahmin-Shudra
37. Brahmin-Vaishya-Kshtriya-Brahmin
38. Brahmin-Vaishya-Kshtriya-Kshtriya
39. Brahmin-Vaishya-Kshtriya-Vaishya
40. Brahmin-Vaishya-Kshtriya-Shudra

41. Brahmin-Vaishya-Vaishya-Brahmin
42. Brahmin-Vaishya-Vaishya-Kshtriya
43. Brahmin-Vaishya-Vaishya-Vaishya
44. Brahmin-Vaishya-Vaishya-Shudra
45. Brahmin-Vaishya-Shudra-Brahmin
46. Brahmin-Vaishya-Shudra-Kshtriya
47. Brahmin-Vaishya-Shudra-Vaishya
48. Brahmin-Vaishya-Shudra-Shudra
49. Brahmin-Shudra-Brahmin-Brahmin
50. Brahmin-Shudra-Brahmin-Kshtriya
51. Brahmin-Shudra-Brahmin-Vaishya
52. Brahmin-Shudra-Brahmin-Shudra
53. Brahmin-Shudra-Kshtriya-Brahmin
54. Brahmin-Shudra-Kshtriya-Kshtriya
55. Brahmin-Shudra-Kshtriya-Vaishya
56. Brahmin-Shudra-Kshtriya-Shudra
57. Brahmin-Shudra-Vaishya-Brahmin
58. Brahmin-Shudra-Vaishya-Kshtriya
59. Brahmin-Shudra-Vaishya-Vaishya
60. Brahmin-Shudra-Vaishya-Shudra
61. Brahmin-Shudra-Shudra-Brahmin
62. Brahmin-Shudra-Shudra-Kshtriya
63. Brahmin-Shudra-Shudra-Vaishya
64. Brahmin-Shudra-Shudra-Shudra
65. **Kshtriya-Brahmin-Brahmin-Brahmin**
66. Kshtriya-Brahmin-Brahmin-Kshtriya
67. Kshtriya-Brahmin-Brahmin-Vaishya
68. Kshtriya-Brahmin-Brahmin-Shudra

69. Kshtriya-Brahmin-Kshtriya-Brahmin
70. Kshtriya-Brahmin-vaishya-Brahmin
71. Kshatriya-Brahmin-Shudra-Brahmin
72. Kshtriya-Brahmin-Kshtriya-Kshtriya
73. Kshtriya-Brahmin-Vaishya-Kshtriya
74. Kshtriya-Brahmin-Shudra-Kshtriya
75. Kshtriya-Brahmin-Kshtriya-Vaishya
76. Kshtriya-Brahmin-Vaishya-Vaishya
77. Kshtriya-Brahmin-Shudra-Vaishya
78. Kshtriya-Brahmin-Kshtriya-Shudra
79. Kshtriya-Brahmin-Vaishya-Shudra
80. Kshtriya-Brahmin-Shudra-Shudra
81. Kshtriya-Kshtriya-Brahmin-Brahmin
82. Kshtriya-Kshtriya-Brahmin-Kshtriya
83. Kshtriya-Kshtriya-Brahmin-Vaishya
84. Kshtriya-Kshtriya-Brahmin-Shudra
85. Kshtriya-Kshtriya-Kshtriya-Brahmin
86. **Kshtriya-Kshtriya-Kshtriya-Kshtriya**
87. Kshtriya -Kshtriya-Kshtriya-Vaishya
88. Kshtriya-Kshtriya-Kshtriya-Shudra
89. Kshtriya-Kshtriya-Vaishya-Brahmin
90. Kshtriya-Kshtriya-Vaishya-Kshtriya
91. Kshtriya-Kshtriya-Vaishya-Vaishya
92. Kshtriya-Kshtriya-Vaishya-Shudra
93. Kshtriya-Kshtriya-Shudra-Brahmin
94. Kshtriya-Kshtriya-Shudra-Kshtriya
95. Kshtriya-Kshtriya-Shudra-Vaishya
96. Kshtriya-Kshtriya-Shudra-Shudra

97. Kshtriya-Vaishya-Brahmin-Brahmin

98. Kshtriya-Vaishya-Brahmin-Kshtriya

99. Kshtriya-Vaishya-Brahmin-Vaishya

100. Kshtriya-Vaishya-Brahmin-Shudra

101. Kshtriya-Vaishya-Kshtriya-Brahmin

102. Kshtriya-Vaishya-Kshtriya-Kshtriya

103. Kshtriya-Vaishya-Kshtriya-Vaishya

104. Kshtriya-Vaishya-Kshtriya-Shudra

105. Kshtriya-Vaishya-Vaishya-Brahmin

106. Kshtriya-Vaishya-Vaishya-Kshtriya

107. Kshtriya-Vaishya-Vaishya-Vaishya

108. Kshtriya-Vaishya-Vaishya-Shudra

109. Kshtriya-Vaishya-Shudra-Brahmin

110. Kshtriya-Vaishya-Shudra-Kshtriya

111. Kshtriya-Vaishya-Shudra-Vaishya

112. Kshtriya-Vaishya-Shudra-Shudra

113. Kshtriya-Shudra-Brahmin-Brahmin

114. Kshtriya-Shudra-Brahmin-Kshtriya

115. Kshtriya-Shudra-Brahmin-Vaishya

116. Kshtriya-Shudra-Brahmin-Shudra

117. Kshtriya-Shudra-Kshtriya-Brahmin

118. Kshtriya-Shudra-Kshtriya-Kshtriya

119. Kshtriya-Shudra-Kshtriya-Vaishya

120. Kshtriya-Shudra-Kshtriya-Shudra

121. Kshtriya-Shudra-Vaishya-Brahmin

122. Kshtriya-Shudra-Vaishya-Kshtriya

123. Kshtriya-Shudra-Vaishya-Vaishya

124. Kshtriya-Shudra-Vaishya-Shudra

125. Kshtriya-Shudra-Shudra-Brahmin
126. Kshtriya-Shudra-Shudra-Kshtriya
127. Kshtriya-Shudra-Shudra-Vaishya
128. Kshatriya-Shudra-Shudra-Shudra
129. **Vaishya-Brahmin-Brahmin-Brahmin**
130. Vaishya-Brahmin-Brahmin-Kshtriya
131. Vaishya-Brahmin-Brahmin-Vaishya
132. Vaishya-Brahmin-Brahmin-Shudra
133. Vaishya-Brahmin-Kshtriya-Brahmin
134. Vaishya-Brahmin-vaishya-Brahmin
135. Vaishya-Brahman-Shudra-Brahmin
136. Vaishya-Brahmin-Kshtriya-Kshtriya
137. Vaishya-Brahmin-Vaishya-Kshtriya
138. Vaishya-Brahmin-Shudra-Kshtriya
139. Vaishya-Brahmin-Kshtriya-Vaishya
140. Vaishya-Brahmin-Vaishya-Vaishya
141. Vaishya-Brahmin-Shudra-Vaishya
142. Vaishya-Brahmin-Kshtriya-Shudra
143. Vaishya-Brahmin-Vaishya-Shudra
144. Vaishya-Brahmin-Shudra-Shudra
145. Vaishya-Kshtriya-Brahmin-Brahmin
146. Vaishya-Kshtriya-Brahmin-Kshtriya
147. Vaishya-Kshtriya-Brahmin-Vaishya
148. Vaishya-Kshatriya-Brahmin-Shudra
149. Vaishya-Kshtriya-Kshtriya-Brahmin
150. Vaishya-Kshtriya-Kshtriya-Kshtriya
151. Vaishya-Kshtriya-Kshtriya-Vaishya
152. Vaishya-Kshtriya-Kshtriya-Shudra

153. Vaishya-Kshtriya-Vaishya-Brahmin
154. Vaishya-Kshtriya-Vaishya-Kshtriya
155. Vaishya-Kshtriya-Vaishya-Vaishya
156. Vaishya-Kshtriya-Vaishya-Shudra
157. Vaishya-Kshtriya-Shudra-Brahmin
158. Vaishya-Kshtriya-Shudra-Kshtriya
159. Vaishya-Kshtriya-Shudra-Vaishya
160. Vaishya-Kshtriya-Shudra-Shudra
161. Vaishya-Vaishya-Brahmin-Brahmin
162. Vaishya-Vaishya-Brahmin-Kshtriya
163. Vaishya-Vaishya-Brahmin-Vaishya
164. Vaishya-Vaishya-Brahmin-Shudra
165. Vaishya-Vaishya-Kshtriya-Brahmin
166. Vaishya-Vaishya-Kshtriya-Kshtriya
167. Vaishya-Vaishya-Kshtriya-Vaishya
168. Vaishya-Vaishya-Kshtriya-Shudra
169. Vaishya-Vaishya-Vaishya-Brahmin
170. Vaishya-Vaishya-Vaishya-Kshtriya
171. **Vaishya-Vaishya-Vaishya-Vaishya**
172. Vaishya-Vaishya-Vaishya-Shudra
173. Vaishya-Vaishya-Shudra-Brahmin
174. Vaishya-Vaishya-Shudra-Kshtriya
175. Vaishya-Vaishya-Shudra-Vaishya
176. Vaishya-Vaishya-Shudra-Shudra
177. Vaishya-Shudra-Brahmin-Brahmin
178. Vaishya-Shudra-Brahmin-Kshtriya
179. Vaishya-Shudra-Brahmin-Vaishya
180. Vaishya-Shudra-Brahmin-Shudra

181. Vaishya-Shudra-Kshtriya-Brahmin
182. Vaishya-Shudra-Kshtriya-Kshtriya
183. Vaishya-Shudra-Kshtriya-Vaishya
184. Vaishya-Shudra-Kshtriya-Shudra
185. Vaishy-Shudra-Vaishya-Brahmin
186. Vaishya-Shudra-Vaishya-Kshtriya
187. Vaishya-Shudra-Vaishya-Vaishya
188. Vaishya-Shudra-Vaishya-Shudra
189. Vaishya-Shudra-Shudra-Brahmin
190. Vaishya-Shudra-Shudra-Kshtriya
191. Vaishya-Shudra-Shudra-Vaishya
192. Vaishya-Shudra-Shudra-Shudra
193. **Shudra-Brahmin-Brahmin-Brahmin**
194. Shudra-Brahmin-Brahmin-Kshtriya
195. Shudra-Brahmin-Brahmin-Vaishya
196. Shudra-Brahmin-Brahmin-Shudra
197. Shudra-Brahmin-Kshtriya-Brahmin
198. Shudra-Brahmin-vaishya-Brahmin
199. Shudra-Brahman-Shudra-Brahmin
200. Shudra-Brahmin-Kshtriya-Kshtriya
201. Shudra-Brahmin-Vaishya-Kshtriya
202. Shudra-Brahmin-Shudra-Kshtriya
203. Shudra-Brahmin-Kshtriya-Vaishya
204. Shudra-Brahmin-Vaishya-Vaishya
205. Shudra-Brahmin-Shudra-Vaishya
206. Shudra-Brahmin-Kshatriya-Shudra
207. Shudra-Brahmin-Vaishya-Shudra
208. Shudra-Brahmin-Shudra-Shudra

209. Shudra-Kshtriya-Brahmin-Brahmin
210. Shudra-Kshtriya-Brahmin-Kshtriya
211. Shudra-Kshtriya-Brahmin-Vaishya
212. Shudra-Kshtriya-Brahmin-Shudra
213. Shudra-Kshtriya-Kshtriya-Brahmin
214. Shudra-Kshtriya-Kshtriya-Kshtriya
215. Shudra-Kshtriya-Kshtriya-Vaishya
216. Shudra-Kshtriya-Kshtriya-Shudra
217. Shudra-Kshtriya-Vaishya-Brahmin
218. Shudra-Kshtriya-Vaishya-Kshtriya
219. Shudra-Kshtriya-Vaishya-Vaishya
220. Shudra-Kshtriya-Vaishya-Shudra
221. Shudra-Kshtriya-Shudra-Brahmin
222. Shudra-Kshtriya-Shudra-Kshtriya
223. Shudra-Kshtriya-Shudra-Vaishya
224. Shudra-Kshatriya-Shudra-Shudra
225. Shudra-Vaishya-Brahmin-Brahmin
226. Shudra-Vaishya-Brahmin-Kshtriya
227. Shudra-Vaishya-Brahmin-Vaishya
228. Shudra-Vaishya-Brahmin-Shudra
229. Shudra-Vaishya-Kshtriya-Brahmin
230. Shudra-Vaishya-Kshtriya-Kshtriya
231. Shudra-Vaishya-Kshtriya-Vaishya
232. Shudra-Vaishya-Kshtriya-Shudra
233. Shudr-Vaishya-Vaishya-Brahmin
234. Shudra-Vaishya-Vaishya-Kshtriya
235. Shudr-Vaishya-Vaishya-Vaishya
236. Shudra-Vaishya-Vaishya-Shudra

237. Shudra-Vaishya-Shudra-Brahmin
238. Shudra-Vaishya-Shudra-Kshtriya
239. Shudra-Vaishya-Shudra-Vaishya
240. Shudr-Vaishya-Shudra-Shudra
241. Shudra-Shudra-Brahmin-Brahmin
242. Shudra-Shudra-Brahmin-Kshtriya
243. Shudra-Shudra-Brahmin-Vaishya
244. Shudra-Shudra-Brahmin-Shudra
245. Shudra-Shudra-Kshtriya-Brahmin
246. Shudra-Shudra-Kshtriya-Kshtriya
247. Shudra-Shudra-Kshtriya-Vaishya
248. Shudra-Shudra-Kshatriya-Shudra
249. Shudra-Shudra-Vaishya-Brahmin
250. Shudra-Shudra-Vaishya-Kshtriya
251. Shudra-Shudra-Vaishya-Vaishya
252. Shudra-Shudra-Vaishya-Shudra
253. Shudra-Shudra-Shudra-Brahmin
254. Shudra-Shudra-Shudra-Kshatriya
255. Shudra-Shudra-Shudra-Vaishya
256. **Shudra-Shudra-Shudra-Shudra**

Various combinations giving various qualities of Children or human beings, needs training as essential similar to Quality comes in Astrology Report.

Sixty four qualities of children taking birth in any specific place depends on their time of birth, parents' quality and their parents' business.

Sometimes places quality also differing in that case in one area 256 types of children will take birth.

This is the activity of society to develop the 256 technology and as per suitability of area to be taught to the Children in Schooling till 17th of age.

5. Naamkaran:-

After the Jatkarma, the naming ceremony is performed.

On the basis of Jyotis , name suggests, the name of the child is kept in it.

The naming ceremony is performed on the 11th day after the birth of the child.

The name of the child is decided according to astrology. Many people name their child whatever is wrong.

It affects his mindset and his future.

Just as wearing good clothes enhances the personality, similarly having a good and concise name has its effect on the whole life.

The thing to keep in mind is that the name of the child should be kept in such a way that he is called or known by that name at home and outside.

6. Nishkraman:-

After this, the Nishkraman ceremony is performed in the fourth month of birth.

The meaning of expulsion is to take out.

Our body is made up of earth, water, fire, air and sky etc. which are called Panchabhutas.

Therefore the father prays to these deities for the welfare of the child.

Also wish the baby a long life and a healthy life.

7. Annaprashan: Annaprashan Sanskar is performed at the time of teething of the child i. e. at the age of 6-7 months.

After this ritual, feeding of food to the child begins. In the beginning, well prepared food like kheer, khichdi, rice etc. is given.

8. Chudakarma: When the hair of the head is removed for the first time, then it is called Chudakarma or Mundan Sanskar.

When the child is one year old, or at the age of three, or at the age of the fifth or seventh year, the child's hair is plucked.

This sanskar strengthens the child's head and sharpens the intellect.

Along with this, the germs sticking in the hair of the baby are destroyed, due to which the baby gets health benefits.

It is believed that after coming out of the womb, only the hair given by the parents remains on the head of the child.

Cutting them leads to purification.

9. Karnavedha : The meaning of Karnavedh Sanskar is piercing the ear.

There are five reasons for this, one- to wear jewelry. Second-Piercing the ear stops the bad effects of Rahu and Ketu according to astrology.

Third, it is acupuncture, due to which the flow of blood in the veins

going to the brain starts to improve.

Fourth, it increases hearing power and prevents many diseases.

Fifth, it strengthens the sexual senses.

10. Yagyopavit:

Yagyopavit is also called 5 to 48 days Upanayan or Janeu Sanskar.

This is the compulsory activity before entering the School.

This is the Sanskar when children get Discipline in their Life.

This is the essential Sanskar for the Strong Democracy.

Every Individual on the basis of their Birth caste performs this sanskar.

Brahmin, Kshtriya and Vaishya who are taking birth to work for society have a compulsory requirement to be the Dwij as their mind is more creative and actionable, hence Guru is essential for them.

The person who is taking birth in Shudra Caste, they are not required to be Dwij, because their birth quality is to Serve the Society in peace as their mind is always in peace. But due to social disharmony these people reached a stage of Avid Yagami(Those who trying to be similar like others)

Upa means to pass and Nayan means to carry.

To be taken to the Guru means to perform the Upanayana ceremony.

There are three, Six and Nine sutras in the Janeu i. e. Yagnopavit.

These are the symbols of three deities- Brahma, Vishnu, Mahesh.

This sanskar gives knowledge of Nature, strength, energy and radiance to the child. At the same time, a spiritual sense is awakened in him.

METHODOLOGY TO PERFORM UPNAYAN SANSKAR

Upnayan Sanskar is an old and Technical Sanskar which can change our Society in the Right Path. A few castes now follow this Sanskar and deliver it to the next Generation.

#Guru, #Asst. Guru & #Sevak must be a SAINT and practical personal and away from all Greeds and who can devote 12 days and Night with Children and teach the Children from 4AM and their age should be 65+and Asst. Guru age be 50+.

GURU must have 10 year experience as a Asst. Guru. Asst. Guru must have experience of min. 10yrs as a SEVAK.

SEVAK must be a person taken Upnayan Sanskar and following discipline from the last 10 years and without Greeds. Minimum age-21 years.

Today we prepared a Guidelines in Stepwise such that we can improve the quality to our future generation, and present generation in Technical aspects such that our vision should run for a long time.

Plan is for a minimum of 11 days with ARYA MOUN, which is essential for UPNAYAN SANSKAR.

DAY-1

Each PARENTS will make Puja of #KULDEVTA in Home and bring their son to Ashram till 2 PM with Light Clothes.

#Ashram will provide suitable Bed, Bed sheet and normal facility at ashram with suitable Chappal/Kharaw to all Children as guidelines of Guru & Asst. Guru.

5PM to 6PM -Dinner .

6PM-7. 45PM- Introduction Classes by Guru & Asst. Guru. Delivery Speech for the programme of Upnayan Sanskar, Discipline of Ashram etc, start of #ARYA MOUN, and Dinner to Honorable Guest.

7. 45PM-8. 15PM-Day & Next day Programme discussion and Sense, Brain & Intellect Pranayam by GURU.

DAY-2

4AM-4. 30AM - Wakeup and Become fresh with Bath. with help of Asst. Guru.

4. 30AM-6. 30AM-Guru Bandana+Sarvangasan Pranayama+Self Surrender Pranayama+LIFE ENERGY PRANAYAM+Sense Brain & Intellect Control Pranayam (Class-I)

6. 30AM-7AM - Breakfast

7AM-11. 00AM - Preparation by Children of Marwa+Matkor+Haldi Kalash in guideline of GURU.

11. 00AM-11. 45AM- Lunch

11. 45AM to 1. 30PM-Rest

1. 30PM -3. 30PM-Organising of Marwa+Matkor+Haldi kalash

3. 30PM-5. 30PM-Starting of Upnayan Sanskar+Ghrit Dhari+Puja of

Satya Narayan Kath. Barua Dressing.

5. 30PM-6. 00PM-Dinner to Barua

6. 00PM-7. 45PM - Bhakti Yog by Barua with GURU+Dinner to Honorable Guest.

7. 45PM -8. 15PM - Day & Next day Programme discussion and Sense, Brain & Intellect Pranayam by GURU.

8. 15PM-4AM - Rest.

DAY-3

4AM-4. 30AM - Wakeup and Become fresh with Bath with help of Asst. Guru.

4. 30AM-6. 30AM-Guru Bandana+Sarvangasan Pranayama+Self Surrender Pranayama+LIFE ENERGY PRANAYAM+Sense Brain & Intellect Control Pranayam (Class-II)

6. 30AM-7AM - Breakfast

7AM-10. 00AM - BHICHHATAN-I(External decided by Guru)

10. 00AM-11. 45AM- Preparation of Food & Lunch by Barua with GURU.

11. 45AM to 1. 30PM-Rest

1. 30PM -3. 00PM-Practice of Self Surrender & Life Energy Pranayama under Asst. Guru. 3. 00PM-4. 30PM-Practice of Sense, Brain & Intellect Pranayama under Asst. Guru.

4. 30PM-6. 00PM-Preparation and Dinner to Barua under Guidance and with GURU.

6. 00PM-7. 45PM - Bhakti Yog by Barua under guidance of GURU+Dinner to Honorable Guest

7. 45PM-8. 15PM- Day & Next day Programme discussion and Self Control Pranayam by GURU.

8. 15PM-4AM-REST

Day-4(Class-III) and BHICHHATAN-II(External decided by GURU), Rest similar as Day-3

Day-5(Class-IV), BICHHAWAN-III(External decided by GURU), Rest similar as Day-3

Day-6(Class-V), BHICHHATAN-IV(External decided by GURU), Rest similar as Day-3

Day-7(Class-VI), BHICHHATAN-V(External decided by GURU), Rest similar as Day-3

Day-8(Class-VII), BHICHHATAN-VI(External decided by GURU), Rest similar as Day-3

Day-9(Class-VIII), BHICHHATAN-VII(External decided byGURU), Rest similar as Day-3

Day-10(Class-IX), BHICHHATAN-VIII (External decided by GURU), Rest similar as Day-3

DAY-11

4AM-4. 30AM - Wakeup and Become fresh with Bath with help of Asst. GURU.

4. 30AM-6. 30AM-SELF CONTROL MEDITATION(Class-X)

6. 30AM-7AM - Breakfast

7AM-10. 00AM - BHICHHATAN-IX from own family

10. 00AM-11. 45AM- Preparation of Food & Lunch by Barua with GURU.

11. 45AM to 1. 30PM-Rest

1. 30PM -4. 30PM-Providing UPNAYAN

SANSKAR to all Barua. (END OF ARYA MOUN)

4. 30PM-6. 00PM-Preparation and Dinner by Barua under Guidance and with GURU.

6. 00PM-7. 45PM - Bhakti Yog by Barua under guidance of

GURU+Dinner to Honorable Guest

7. 45PM-8. 15PM- Day & Next day Programme and Self Control Pranayam by GURU.

8. 15PM-4AM-Rest.

DAY-12

4AM-4. 30AM - Wakeup and Become fresh with Bath without help of Asst. GURU.

4. 30AM-6. 30AM-SELF CONTROL MEDITATION(Class-XI)

6. 30AM-7AM - Breakfast

7AM-9. 00AM - Group Photographs and Discourse.

PARENTS WILL TAKE CARE OF CHILDREN.

END OF PROGRAMME

11. Vedarambh & Education: Under this the knowledge of Vedas is given to the person. After Veda knowledge people get knowledge of their Birth Caste activity to strengthen the Economics of their family and Society. Practical schooling is required in society to train the student in the right direction before 17 years of age.

Every student must get an offer from the Society or Government of 1 year training with Job offer. Those who are not interested will get support from the Society or Government to start the Business. Those who are interested in further study can go for further study, Society or Government will support them.

12. Samavartan: Samavartan Sanskar means to return again

After receiving education from the ashram or gurukul, this sanskar was performed to bring the person back into the society.

It means preparing a celibate person psychologically for the struggles of life.

13. Marriage & Economic Life: It is necessary to get married at an appropriate age. Marriage ceremony is considered to be the most important sacrament. Under this, both the bride and the groom stay together and get

married, taking a vow to follow the right path in front of Agni and water. Agni is the symbol of truth and purity. Water who remembers the things for a long time.

On the basis of Date of Birth, Place and Time the kundli Milan is the Ist step, after a matching marriage ceremony is held.

Marriage does not only contribute to the development of the universe, but it is also necessary for the spiritual and mental development of a person.

By this sanskar a person is also freed from the debt of the ancestors.

Marriage is also leading and strengthening their Economic Life.

Economic Life starting when Marriage takes place or when Men Women living together. Social Needs developing like organized Food, Water, Environment, Work and safety. Every activity needs valuable time to Perform. Economy starting from Women, as women has capacity to produce the children.

14. Vanaprastha-It provides useful guidelines for peaceful departure from this world where the person comes for a limited period with a certain purpose.

ROUTINE-

1. Barefoot walking to a different TIRTH is the routine for this life.

2. Wake Up early in the morning at 4am.

3. Normally daily 12 KOS or 32 kilometer walking daily morning hour till 11am.

4. Eating twice Vegetarian food once before 12PM and 2nd before sunset.

5. Staying in a Temple or Ashram.

6. Performing morning puja and evening Meditation and some time talking with the public in afternoon time.

It is one's duty to pass on the mantle to the future generation without any attachment to one's own position.

It increases the Mangal Maitri.

15. SANYAS ASHRAM-

In Hinduism(SANATAN) renunciation or sanyasa is the true mark of spiritual life.

It is believed to be the simple and straightforward way to achieve moksha or liberation.

Truly speaking, in the context of sanyasa or renunciation, the word, "achieve, " is not the right word to use because "achieve" denotes materialism, seeking and striving for something, whereas in renunciation one has to give up worldly life and material possessions, and live without aiming for anything in particular, including the goal of salvation, liberation or union with God.

Having a purpose is important in worldly life, whereas not having any purpose is the central feature of renunciation or sannyasa in Hinduism.

A step which is the final path to increase the Mangal Maitri. His family is whole Nature.

TYPES OF SANYAS AND WORK-

Different types of Sanyas in the world are as under.

A. MONK B. Mandir Pujari C. Saint and performing Meditation in one place D. Saint and traveling to Tirth . D. Saint and performing meditation to construct the State or Country. E. Munni F. Father G. Saint and performing meditation and running school, Temple and Health Center.

16. Activity After Death or Funeral rites -

There is three activity after Death is as under-

1. When Arihant takes Samadhi, it is required to be put under the Earth or Water Samadhi or Well Samadhi or Forest Samadhi as desired by Arihant.

2. When a Child takes Death, it is required to be put under the Earth.

3. Normal people who get death due to poor health or by accident or else the dead body is offered to the Fire.

Thus sixteen sacraments are performed. ,

Antyashti Sanskar means funeral. After the death of a person i. e. renouncing the body, the dead body is offered to the fire.

Even today before the funeral procession, a fire is taken from the house by burning it.

DEVOTION-

Bhakti is the foundation of all Work and spiritual practice. It is both a means and an end in itself. What is the nature of Bhakti or Work? The Narada Bhakti Sutras say: 'It is of the nature of supreme love towards **God**' (2nd Sutra).

Nine Ways of Devotion (Navadha Bhakti)

How does this love towards the divine manifest itself? The Srimad **Bhagavatam**, delineates the nine ways (Navadha Bhakti or Work) in which we can lovingly connect with God:

1). Hearing about God (Shravana)

2). Chanting His Name and Glory (**Kirtana)**

3). Remembering Him (Smarana)

4). Serving His Lotus Feet (Pada Sevana)

5). Worshiping Him as per the Scriptures (Archana)

6). Prostrating before Him (Vandana)

7). Being His Servant (Dasya)

8). Befriending Him (Sakhya)

9). Offering Oneself to Him (Atma Nivedana)

1). Hearing about God (Shravana):

Listening to His divine name, His divine form, His Qualities, Actions, Mysteries etc. , and getting lost in His glorious Lila is known as Shravana. Should we hear about God? Shri **Krishna** says in the **Gita**: "You can get that knowledge by humbly prostrating yourself before a Jnani Guru"

Mahamuni Shukadeva Narrating Bhagavata Purana to Raja Parikshata

Therefore, the first step in Shravana is to take recourse at the feet of a Guru. The Shravana aspect of Bhakti is exemplified most completely in King Parikshit, who listened to the Srimad Bhagavatam from the great sage Shukadeva. What effect did this listening have on Parikshit? At the end he said: "Respected Sukhdev Ji, you have made me experience the highest, fearless state. As a consequence I am now totally at peace. I am not afraid of death; let it come to me in any form now. I am totally fearless (Abhaya)" .

2). Chanting His Name and Glory (Kirtana):

Kirtana consists of chanting aloud God's divine name and glories of His form, His qualities, Mysteries, and Lilas; and, in the process of chanting, experiencing extreme thrill culminating in tears and a lightening of the heart.

Reconstructing Devotion Through Narada Bhakti Sutra

The very embodiment of Kirtana is the revered sage Narada. In fact, so engrossed is Narada in the act of Kirtana that he was actually happy when a curse was placed on him that he would not be able to stay in one place and would have to roam around the three worlds. Instead of lamenting this curse, he welcomed it saying that it would enable him to spread the Lord's name and glory all over the three worlds.

3). Remembering Him (Smarana):

Smarana means the constant remembrance of God. Krishna says in the Bhagavad Gita:

"The one who sees Me in everything and everything in Me, I am always present for him and he is always present for Me"

"Therefore, always keep Me in mind and then enter the battle of life. Undoubtedly you will attain unto me".

"The one who does not ruminate on anything else but constantly remembers me only, he finds it easy to reach Me".

As per the Srimad Bhagavatam:

"The mind which thinks of material objects becomes attached to those very objects. However, the mind which constantly remembers me, merges into Me"

Narasimha Drags Down The King Hiranyakashipu

An inspiring example of Smarana is Prahlada, who due to his constant remembrance of God was able to perceive Him everywhere. In fact, when his evil father ridiculed him saying that if God was everywhere, why did He not show up in the pillar in front of them? The father then kicked the pillar, out of which sprang Lord Narasimha, validating the truth of Prahlada's conviction. .

4). Serving His Lotus Feet (Pada Sevana):

The Srimad Bhagavatam says: 'Only till we have not taken recourse to the lotus feet of the Lord is there any cause of concern from money, family etc, which otherwise are a cause of fear and Dukha

Shesha Shayi Vishnu in Yoga Nidra

The obvious example of this kind of Bhakti is our mother **goddess Lakshmi,** who is seen in constant service of Lord **Vishnu's** lotus feet.

5). Worshiping Him as per the Scriptures (Archana):

Archana consists of the physical worship of God in the form of an idol etc, using the correct rituals (upacharas) as prescribed in the scriptures. These **rituals** consist of procedures like bathing and clothing the Deity, and also offering Him scents, **food** etc. An essential requirement of Archana is the presence of faith (Shraddha) in the devotee. As Shri Krishna puts it in the Gita: "Whatever is offered to me, whether it be a leaf, flower, fruit or water, if it is done with Bhakti, I accept it".

Srimad Bhagavata: The Holy Book of God (Set of 4 Volumes)

An example of Archana Bhakti is that of King Prithu in the Srimad Bhagavatam, who satisfied Shri Vishnu with the selfless Vedic sacrifices he performed, so much so that the Lord presented Himself in person before the king.

6). Prostrating before Him (Vandana):

Vandana means prostrating oneself before the Lord. An illuminating example of this Bhakti is Akrura, another great personality in the Srimad Bhagavatam. The great Bhakta Akrura could not contain himself when he entered Vrindavana. He was overcome with emotion and the consequent surge of affection for Krishna made his hair stand on its end and the overflowing eyes began to shed tears. Akrura jumped onto the land of Vrindavana and rolled around on the earth saying: "Oh! This is the dust touched by the feet of my beloved Lord".

On going further, he saw Krishna milking the cows. The physical beauty of the Lord overwhelmed Akrura so much that he rushed down and prostrated himself at the feet of Krishna. Understanding Akrura's mental state, Krishna helped him to his feet, drew him to His heart and then embraced His beloved devotee".

7). Being His Servant (Dasya):

Being in selfless service of God, fulfilling His intentions and unquestioningly obeying all His orders is known as Dasya. The most powerful embodiment of this kind of Bhakti is undoubtedly Shri **Hanuman**, who as soon as he caught a glimpse of Shri **Rama**, declared himself to be the latter's servant.

Sri Rama Bhakta Hanuman Ji

Being a servant of God means leaving aside one's most important work to respectfully do the Lord's bidding; leaving all of one's own desires to fulfill His desire; considering even the greatest effort done for Him to be miniscule; thinking His ownership over our body to be greater than even our own; understanding that our wealth, life, body etc is useful only as long as it is in the use of God and so on. Hanuman had all these qualities, and no wonder that Shri Rama embraced him saying: "You are more dear to me than even Lakshmana" (**Ramayana of Tulsidas**).

8). Befriending Him (Sakhya):

Sakhya means personal friendship with God, a friendship in which there is a constant desire to stay in His company, and one enjoys conversations only with Him, and becomes extremely pleased on the mere mention of one's friend from a third person. Krishna Himself tells us who His friend is: "O Arjuna, you are both my friend and Bhakta".

The Mahabharata

Stories about the friendship of Krishna and Arjuna abound in the **Mahabharata** and Bhagavatam. Narratives show how they indulged in light banter, sports etc, which provide us with ample glimpses into the nature of their mutual friendship.

9). Offering Oneself to Him (Atma Nivedana):

Offering oneself wholly, including all of one's material possessions, with firm conviction, is known as Atmanivedana. The example of such surrender is king Bali, who was asked by an adolescent Brahmin for a piece of land equivalent to the distance measured by the latter's three footsteps. The Brahmin, who was none other than the Vamana Avatara of Lord Vishnu, measured out all the worlds with only two of His steps and finally there remained nowhere to place the promised third.

Vamana Purana with Hindi Translation

Seeing that there was no place left for Vamana's last step, Bali, bowing before Him, requested Him to place it on his head. In the end, after having thus given up everything, did the king feel any remorse or bitterness? No. In fact, this is what he said: "Thank you God for your grace. Indeed, when we become blind with pride due to our wealth, you, by taking away our money, give us back our eyes" (Srimad Bhagavatam 8. 22. 5). This was the glorious Bali who gave up his all to the Lord.

Jharokha (Window) Painted with King Bali Pledging Himself to Vamana Avatar of Vishnu

Conclusion:

These are the nine ways in which we can relate to God. We are free to select the particular connection with God which suits our personal temperament. However remember that all these nine qualities existed together in the Bhaktas mentioned above. Did Arjuna not have Pada Sevana, Smarana etc? Of course he did. For us this means that once we have imbibed even one of these virtues properly, all others will follow suit, and the person becomes a Shuddha Bhakta, one whose each and every action can be deemed as Bhakti.

Ashrams

Ashram means "a place of Work or spiritual shelter. " Each stage of life is not only a natural part of the journey from cradle to grave, but a time at which spirituality can be developed. The four *varnas*, accept *ashrams* as depicted in the table below:

	BRAHM ACARI	GRIHASTA	VANA PRASTHA	SANNYASI
Shudra	no formal education	yes	no formal retirement	no formal sannyasa
Vaishya	yes	yes	no formal retirement	no formal sannyasa
Kshatriya	yes	yes	yes	no formal sannyasa
Brahmin	yes	yes	yes	yes

Today, only a few Hindus strictly follow all these four *ashrams*. Nonetheless, the idea of enjoying the world in a religious and regulated manner, followed by gradual retirement remains a powerful ideal.

Each of the four *ashrams* has its specific duties. The main ones are listed below.

Brahmachari (Student Life)

The *brahmachari-ashram*, often away from the home (somewhat like a boarding school), was primarily intended for fostering spiritual values. Memorisation and skill development were subsidiary to character formation and self-realization. Even sons of the royal family were expected to undergo this austere and rigorous training.

To be celibate and live a simple life, free from sense pleasure and material allurement.

To serve the guru (spiritual teacher) and collect alms for him.

To hear, study and assimilate the Vedas.

To develop all the appropriate qualities: humility, discipline, simplicity, purity of thought, cleanliness, soft-heartedness, and so on.

Grihasta (Household Life)

Traditionally some men remained lifelong celibates, either remaining as *brahmacharis* or immediately becoming *sannyasis*. Others were required to marry, extending their responsibilities to include wives, children, relatives, and society in general. This *ashram* is the only one permitting sexual gratification.

- ❑ To make money and to enjoy sensual pleasure according to ethical principles.
- ❑ To perform sacrifice and observe religious rituals.
- ❑ To protect and nourish family members (wife, children, and elders).
- ❑ To teach children spiritual values.
- ❑ To give in charity, and especially to feed holy people, the poor, and animals.

Vanaprastha (Retired Life)

After the children have left home and settled, a man may gradually retire from family responsibilities and, with his wife, begin to focus his mind on spiritual matters. Often he goes on pilgrimage. His wife may accompany him, but all sexual relationships are forbidden. *Vanaprashta* literally means "forest-dweller."

- ❑ To generally devote more time to spiritual matters.
- ❑ To engage in austerity and penance.
- ❑ To go on pilgrimage.

Sannyasa (Renounced Life)

This position is traditionally available only to men who exhibit the qualities of a *brahmana*. The man would leave home and family and was prohibited from seeing his wife again. Considered civilly dead, he was free to wander, living a life dependent on God alone. The *sannyasis* are conspicuous in their saffron dress. They are often called *sadhus* (holy people) – To fully control the mind and senses, and to fix the mind on the

Supreme.

- ❑ To become detached and fearless, fully dependent on God as the only protector.
- ❑ To teach and preach the importance of self-realization and God-consciousness, especially to the householders, who often become distracted from their spiritual duties.

Meaning and Purpose

- ❑ What does the system of four ashrams say about the purpose of life, according to Hindu thought?

Personal Reflection

- ❑ Do these stages resemble what happens in other societies? If so, what are the similarities? What are the differences?
- ❑ Are there any values which stand out for us, or with which we strongly agree or disagree? Why?
- ❑ How is our evaluation of these practices coloured by our own world view and our own culture and upbringing.
- ❑ Why does democracy need education?
- ❑ The hallmark of democracy is that it permits citizens to participate in making laws and public policies by regularly choosing their leaders and by voting in assemblies or referendums. If their participation is to be meaningful and effective—if the democracy is to be real and not a sham—citizens must understand their own interests, know the relevant facts, and have the ability to critically evaluate political arguments. Each of those things presupposes education.

Methodology to be Ayurvedic Sanatan Hindu Rastra Akhand Bharat/World-2050

Creation of Ayurvedic Sanatan Hindu Rastra Akhand Bharat/World should be a Mission.

Chanakya created an environment to increase the Land by Drive and by drive Chanakya, successfully completed the Mission Akhand Bharat.

Their mission was to teach the children in Gurukul after getting Upnayan Sanskar or School itself organizing the Upnayan Sanskar before entering the school.

Teaching 25 types of Technology such that every student should become self dependent.

Study as 1. Metallergy 2. Flight 3. Navigation 4. Space Science 5. Enviornment 6. Solar Study 7. Lunar Study 8. Weather Forecast 9. Battery 10. Solar Energy 11. Technology of Day & Night 12. Space Research 13. Astronomy 14. Geography 15. Time 16. Geology and mining 17. Gravity 18. Solar Energy 19. Gems and Metals 20. Communication 21. Plane 22. Water vessels 23. Arms and Ammunitions 24. Zoology & Botany 25. Yagya or Material Science.

Gurukul also teaching the 25 no. Commercial Education is as under-

1. Commerce 2. Agriculture 3. Animal Husbandry 4. Bird Keeping 5. Animal Training 6. Mechanics 7. Vehicle Designing 8. Gems 9. Jewellery Designing 10. Textile 11. Pottery 12. Metallurgy 13. Takshak 14. Dying 15. Khatawkar 16. Logistics 17. Architect 18. Cooking 19. Driving 20.

Water Management 21. Data Entry 22. Animal Husbandry 23. Horticulture 24. Paramedical 25. Forestry Horticulture.

Region of Ashoka arose, he followed the Buddha Technology of Peace on stage when he was in full power.

World saw the result, Akhand Bharat converted in various parts because people tried to follow the Technology of Peace and changed the Mind of decrease to unite the Country.

To Learn as a Lesson in present condition Bharat has to respect the past technology. Following methodology can change the system and create the Akhand Bharat.

Step-1 Strengthen the Schooling with implementation of Gurukul System and teach the discipline of life before or at time joining the School or Gurukul.

Government have a single mission to follow the Sixteen Sanskar from Birth to Death.

Step-2 There is a Workshop needed in every School, College and

University of 16 sanskar, 4 Life of Ashram and Navdha Bhakti (Karma) and Practical teaching of Vipassana Technology with Anapana and Mangal Maitri for peace for Girls and Women.

Step-3 After implementation of above for a minimum of 6 years, Bharat will reach to the extreme and the other country will think of joining Bharat by itself to observe the Discipline and Economic Position of AYURVEDIC SANATAN HINDU RASTRA BHARAT.

Step-4 After 12 years of implementation maturity will take place and the rest of the country which is the real part of Akhand Bharat will join the hand to the Akhand Bharat.

Step-5 As time will run, most of the public in the Country will follow the rules of Janewdhari and develop in economic issue. Bharat will become number-1 in Economy.

Step-6 Slowly slowly the rest of the country will accept the Discipline and Join the Country. Even World will follow the Discipline and Economic Theory of AYURVEDIC SANATAN HINDU RASTRA BHARAT.

Step-7 Not only Ayurvedic Sanatan Hindu Rastra Akhand Bharat will form, even Ayurvedic Sanatan Hindu Rastra Akhand Vishwa will form.

Findings and Further Study

There is now a condition arising to study how to reach the NUMBER ONE ECONOMIC CONDITION in the world, needs further Study.

How Women are the reason for START OF ECONOMY needs further deep study.